# Nothing's Wrong

*(Except Maybe Everything)*

*by*

*Debra Prince*

ISBN:

Ebook: 979-8-90224-046-4

Paperback: 979-8-90224-047-1

Hardcover: 979-8-90224-048-8

**Published by:**

*Authors Publishing House*

178 Broadway, 3rd Floor, #1343

New York, NY 10001, USA

**Main Line:** (855) 624-0155

**Email:** support@authorspublishinghouse.com

# Table of Contents

# Dedication

For my daughter, Sabrina, a teacher whose heart makes room for every child. Thank you for noticing the quiet ones, lifting the unsure ones, and giving every student a voice that matters.

# Acknowledgments

This book is dedicated to every child who has ever felt unseen, unheard, or quietly standing in the corner of their own story, to the ones who keep their feelings tucked in small pockets because they don't want to make life harder for anyone. I see you.

# About the Author

Hi, I'm Debbie Prince, and I'm so glad you're here. I've spent many years as a teacher and a helper to kids of all kinds—kids who think in bright colors, kids who feel big feelings, kids who learn in their own wonderful way, and kids who are still figuring themselves out (which is all of us!).

I write stories because I believe every child has a light inside them, a brave, gentle, shining light, and sometimes all we need is a story to remind us it's there.

I love using imagination to help kids feel understood. In my books, you'll find things like heartstrings, glowpetals, calm-down ideas, and magical little moments that help characters feel seen, supported, and strong.

And guess what? As you read, those moments are meant for you, too.

Whether you are a quiet thinker, a big feeler, a great friend, an awesome sibling, or someone still growing into who you are... I wrote this story with you in mind.

Thanks for reading.

I'm cheering for you—always.

— Debbie

*Monday, sitting on the porch swing with a juice box.*

# The Waffle Thing

This morning started with screaming. Not mine.

Benji's.

He woke up and realized there were only two waffles left in the box. He needs three. Every time. Not two. Not four. Always three. That's just how his brain works. I don't really get it, but I know the rules. We all do.

Except Mom forgot to buy more.

So Benji started yelling. Loud. Like, window-shaking loud.

I stayed in bed because I knew what would happen next. Dad rushing in, saying, "It's okay, buddy." Mom trying to fix it. And Benji, yelling the same thing over and over: "THREE WAFFLES. THREE WAFFLES. THREE WAFFLES."

I could hear the dog barking, too. Great start to the day.

Eventually, I got up. Benji was still on the kitchen floor, holding his ears. Mom was counting with him to calm him down. Dad was burning toast. Everyone looked tired.

So I made a fake waffle.

I found a frozen pancake in the back of the freezer, cut it into a circle, and stacked it with the other two. Benji stared at it for a while, like he was scanning it with his brain. Then he nodded and ate all three.

Nobody said thanks. But they never do.

It's not that they don't care. I think they just... forget. Because I'm the "easy one." The big sister. The helper. The one who doesn't yell.

But sometimes I want to yell, too. Not at Benji. Just... at *everything*.

I'm not mad at him. I love him. I really do. But it's hard, and I don't know where to put that feeling. So I guess I'm putting it here.

In this notebook.

Because I'm tired.

And I want someone—*anyone*—to notice that I'm here, too.

—Maya

*Tuesday, sitting on the porch swing with a juice box.*

# My Family Is a Math Problem

I was thinking about Benji and waffles and how nobody ever says thank you, and then I started thinking about math.

Benji *loves* math. It's like his whole life is one big equation. He even says numbers make more sense than people, and honestly? I kind of agree.

So I tried to turn my family into a math problem. It looked like this:

Mom + Dad + Benji = CONSTANT CHAOS

(Then there's me.)

Except I don't really fit into the equation.

Benji is the one everyone's paying attention to. Mom is always Googling things about sensory stuff and autism therapies. Dad works all day and then spends most evenings helping Benji with routines, or fixing things Benji broke by accident, or driving him to special appointments.

And then there's me.

I'm not loud. I don't break things. I don't have meltdowns. I just kind of... do what I'm supposed to.

And it's like that makes me invisible.

Here's how I wrote it in my notebook just now:

Benji = brilliant + difficult

Mom = tired × 100

Dad = quiet + stressed

Me = (there but not important)

I know that sounds dramatic. I don't mean it in a poor-me kind of way. I just don't know where I fit.

Sometimes I wonder what would happen if I messed up on purpose. Like, what if I refused to go to school for no reason? Would everyone suddenly look at me?

Then I feel bad for even thinking that.

Because I know Benji doesn't *want* to be the way he is. His brain just works differently. And he's not trying to steal attention.

Still... sometimes I wish I could have just a little of it back. Just enough to feel like I count, too.

—Maya

*Wednesday 4:15 p.m., lying on the trampoline in the backyard, it's not bouncing, just thinking...*

# Zora Says I'm Allowed

I told Zora I started writing in this journal.

Well... I didn't *tell* her. I kind of hinted at it while we were walking home from the library. I said, "Do you ever just want to say stuff but not actually say it out loud?"

And she goes, "You mean like a journal? Welcome to my world."

Zora always says stuff like that like she's been waiting for me to catch up.

I said I felt kind of guilty writing some of it down. You know, about Benji. Because I *do* love him, and I *do* know it's not his fault. And I *do* know I'm lucky to have a family and a house and a brother who's healthy and all of that.

But sometimes, I think things I'm not supposed to think. Like:

- "Why does everything have to be about Benji?"
- "What if I said I was sad—would anyone even notice?"
- "Is it wrong to want to *not* deal with this every single day?"

Zora didn't flinch. She just nodded and said,

"You're allowed to feel stuff, Maya. You don't have to be the family sponge."

That made me laugh. Sponge. Like I soak up everybody else's mess and just sit there, soggy and quiet.

She's right, though.

So I'm going to keep writing in here. Even the ugly parts. Even the confusing ones. Because I think if I don't let this stuff out, I'll explode. And I'm not really a screaming-in-the-kitchen type of person.

I'm a writing-in-a-notebook-on-a-trampoline type of person, which maybe a little weird. But weird feels better than invisible.

Also, side note: Benji came outside earlier while I was writing and sat on the edge of the trampoline. He didn't say anything. He just lined up five acorns and stared at them like they were doing a dance.

I didn't say anything either. We just sat there for a while. And it wasn't bad.

Not at all.

—Maya

*Thursday morning, writing this before school because it's still sitting in my chest.*

# Almost

Yesterday in language arts, we had a "Get to Know You" partner sheet.

I got paired with Harper. She's nice, in a smart-and-shiny way. Her pencil case has neat little compartments, and she always has extra lead.

One of the questions was, "What's one thing most people don't know about you?"

Harper went first. She said she has a cousin who's a magician, and she's learning card tricks. She even had a deck in her backpack.

Then it was my turn.

And I thought I could tell her. Not everything. Just one thing. One real thing.

Like:

"I have a little brother who's autistic."

Or:

"My house is always loud, even when no one's talking." Or maybe just:

"It's hard sometimes."

I opened my mouth. But the words tangled up. I just said, *"I play piano. Sort of."*

Which isn't even true. I quit last year.

Harper nodded and wrote it down. Then we moved to the next question. I don't know why it's so hard to say real things.

I think I'm afraid people won't know what to do with them. Or maybe they'll try to make me feel better, and it'll just make me feel worse.

So instead, I stay quiet. Or I say "piano."

And then I write the real answer here.

"It's hard sometimes."

There. I said it.

—Maya

*Friday after school (and after the whole "store thing"), in my room with the door closed, feeling still kind of shaky.*

# Benji + Public Places = Chaos

Today was… rough.

We went to the store after school because Mom forgot to buy allergy medicine and sandwich bread and like five other things. I didn't want to go. I had math homework. But Benji had to come too, because Dad had a late work call, and *he can't stay home alone,* obviously.

It started off okay. Benji was calm. He brought his calculator, which is his comfort object right now. (Last month it was a cardboard tube. Don't ask.)

But then— *then*—the fire alarm went off.

Just a test. One of those quick beeps that lasts three seconds. I barely flinched. Benji screamed.

I mean, screamed.

He dropped the calculator. He covered his ears. He dropped to the floor and started kicking. People stared. Someone asked if he was hurt. One lady actually said, *"He shouldn't be out in public if he's going to act like that."*

I wanted to say something. I wanted to scream *right back at her.*

But I just froze.

Mom knelt down with Benji and tried to calm him down, whispering his numbers. "Six, four, two, zero, six, four, two, zero..." like a song. I stood next to the bananas and felt like my whole face was buzzing.

I didn't know if I was mad or embarrassed or sad or just *done*. I kept thinking: Everyone is looking at us.

And also: No one knows what it's like.

They don't know Benji's scared of loud sounds because his ears don't have a "volume knob." They don't know he didn't *choose* to freak out. And they definitely don't know how it feels to be the sister just standing there, invisible but also *on display*.

Later, in the car, Mom said, "Thank you for being patient, sweetheart."

I nodded.

But I wanted to say:

"I don't want to be patient. I want to be able to *not* be patient. I want someone else to handle it for once. I want to cry too."

But of course I didn't.

I just sat there and watched Benji press the calculator buttons in perfect rhythm: 1, 1, 2, 3, 5, 8, 13... (Fibonacci sequence. His favorite.)

Maybe it calmed him down.

But it made me feel like I was disappearing.

—Maya

*Sunday night, 9:02 p.m., under my blanket with a flashlight, no one knows I'm still awake.*

# Mom Thinks I'm Fine

Tonight I accidentally heard something I wasn't supposed to.

I was walking down the hallway to ask Mom if we had more glue sticks (for my poster project), and I heard her talking to Dad in the kitchen. Their voices were low. Not whispering, but serious. The kind of serious that makes you stop walking.

Dad said something like,

"I'm worried he's getting more anxious again. The head-banging, the flapping, it's worse this week."

They were talking about Benji. Mom sighed, then said,

"I know. But we're doing the best we can. At least we don't have to worry about Maya. She's doing great."

That was it.

I backed away before they saw me. I didn't ask about the glue stick. I just went to my room and sat on my bed and felt... weird.

Because here's the thing:

I'm not doing great.

I get good grades, sure. I don't break stuff. I help when I'm asked. But that doesn't mean everything inside me is sunshine and rainbows and perfectly labeled feelings.

Sometimes I feel like there's this version of me that only exists in their heads. She's calm. Responsible. Fine. Always fine.

But what about the *real* me?

The one who sometimes cries into her pillow because she feels invisible.

The one who walks around with a smile even when she's tired of being the "helper." The one who writes in this notebook because it's the only place she can say the truth out loud.

I'm not mad at Mom. I get it. Benji takes a lot of energy. A *lot*. But I still wish she'd asked. Just once.

"Hey, Maya, are you okay?"

I would've told her no.

Not in a falling-apart kind of way.

Just in a real way.

—Maya

*Monday afternoon, the cafeteria was loud today, not noise-loud, people-loud.*

# Other People's Lunch Tables

Sometimes I look around the lunchroom and wonder what it's like to have a quiet brain.

Like, do some people sit down at their table and only think about pizza and juice and who they're sitting next to? Because I sit down and think about all the things.

Benji had a rough morning. He got stuck picking between his red and blue socks and ended up needing the green ones, but they were in the dirty pile. That kind of thing can send the whole house sideways. I got my own lunch packed, double-checked my math homework, and made sure his noise-canceling headphones were in his backpack.

By the time I sat down in the cafeteria, my brain was tired. My table was full. Everyone was talking about a show I haven't seen and laughing about something that happened in gym. I laughed too, even though I didn't really know what was funny.

No one at my table asked about my morning. Or noticed I was quiet. And I didn't say anything because, I mean... what would I even say?

"Hey, my brother had a sock meltdown this morning and my mom forgot I had a quiz today. Want to trade fruit cups?"

Yeah. No.

I don't blame them. They're not mean.

They just don't know what it's like to always be the background character.

I wish sometimes I could switch spots. Just once.

Be the one who gets asked how my day's going first. Be the one someone makes space for.

But I don't say that out loud.

I just write it here.

—Maya

*Tuesday afternoon, sitting on my floor with my homework untouched, I can't stop thinking about what Benji said.*

# The Pattern in the Floor

Okay, so something strange happened today. Not "screaming-in-the-store" strange. More like... *Benji-being-Benji* strange, but different.

It started when I saw him at school. (We go to the same school, but he's in the 5th-grade hallway and I'm in middle school now, obviously.)

He was standing near the big stairwell, staring at the floor like it had just insulted him. His aide was next to him, talking gently like she always does:

"Benji, it's time to go back to class. Can you walk with me now?"

But he didn't move. He just kept looking down. I walked past and gave him a little wave. He didn't wave back—no surprise—but then he said something I didn't expect.

He said:

"It's too loud here. The floor's not right." The aide looked confused. I stopped walking. She said, "Do you mean *you* feel overwhelmed?"

Benji said, "No. The floor is loud. The floor sounds wrong." That's all he said.

I kept walking because I didn't know what else to do. But I've been thinking about it ever since. Because the thing is... that stairwell *does* feel weird.

Like when you walk on it, the ground sort of thumps under your feet, like it's hollow or something. I thought it was just me being dramatic.

But now I'm wondering...

What if Benji noticed something real?

What if he's not just being "sensitive" or "quirky" or whatever word adults use when they don't understand him?

What if his brain is actually picking up on things no one else can? I don't know. Maybe I'm reading too much into it.

So... I went back to that stairwell at school.

The one Benji said was "too loud" and "wrong."

I know it sounds dumb. I mean, it's a floor. Floors aren't supposed to be anything except... there. But ever since he said it, I couldn't stop thinking about it. The way he stood there frozen, like something under his feet was alive. The way he wouldn't move until someone basically dragged him away.

So after the last period, I told Zora I had to grab a paper I dropped and took the long way down. The hallway was almost empty. The light in that stairwell is weird—sort of flickery, even though it's not broken.

I walked down one step at a time, slow. I didn't know what I was looking for. I just... wanted to *feel* what he felt.

And you know what? It did feel different.

Not broken. Not dangerous. Just... strange. Like the floor had a tiny echo, or like the air was heavier right there. When I jumped a little (just once), the floor gave a tiny bit under my feet. I think. Maybe I imagined it.

It's probably nothing.

But also—why did Benji notice it?

He doesn't lie. He doesn't make stuff up. His brain just *notices* things no one else sees. Sometimes that's annoying, like when he counts my spaghetti noodles or tells me my shoelaces are uneven. But sometimes it makes me wonder...

What else is he picking up that we all miss?

I'm not saying I believe the floor is broken. But something about it has Benji's brain *buzzing*. That usually means something's off—even if the rest of us can't feel it yet. I don't know what to do about that.

So for now, I'm just writing it down. And maybe I'll go back again tomorrow. Just to be sure.

I didn't know if it mattered yet, but it stayed in the back of my mind.

—Maya

September 28th

*Wednesday afternoon, writing fast before I forget how it felt.*

# Announcement, and Then Nothing

This morning started off with an announcement over the loudspeaker:

"Our first school dance is coming up! October 4th! All 6th, 7th, and 8th graders are invited!"

Everyone in class immediately started whispering and giggling and fake-screaming, like it was the best news in the world. I felt that fluttery feeling in my stomach—excited but nervous at the same time.

It's not like I've ever been to a dance.

But still, the idea of it. Dressing up. Being with friends. Maybe even just standing in the corner laughing at everything.

I turned to look for Zora. She had that half-smile she does when she's trying not to look too interested. We made eye contact. I thought for sure we'd talk about it at lunch.

But we didn't.

Zora ate lunch at a different table today.

I know that sounds small. It *is* small. But it felt big.

She sat with her math group—Lila and Destiny and those kids who always know all the answers before the question is even done. It wasn't mean or anything. She waved at me. But she didn't come sit with me.

I sat at the end of our usual bench. The side with the wobbly leg. I kept waiting for her to slide over and say, "You looked lonely without me," like she usually does. She didn't.

And I didn't get to talk to her about the dance.

Or tell her how nervous I already am about whether I'll go. Or what I'd wear.

Or how I hope we both go and we don't leave each other alone, even for a second. And then my thoughts just spiraled.

What if she's planning to go with someone else? What if she likes her new group better than me?

What if I'm too much? Or too boring? Or just not enough?

The thing is, I'm not mad at her. I don't even blame her.

I'm tired of being the quiet one. The one who doesn't *need* people to sit with her or check in or notice. Except I do. I do need that. I just don't want to *ask* for it.

Because if I ask and they don't show up, it'll feel worse than being ignored. I think that's one of the hardest parts.

I'm not mad at anyone. But it still hurts.

Maybe Zora was just being friendly. Maybe she thought I needed space. Or maybe it was nothing.

But I still felt like something small cracked a little bit in my chest today. The kind of crack you don't tell anyone about.

You just carry it for a while.

—Maya

*Thursday morning, sitting in the living room at my home with my notebook open but not really writing my warm-up.*

# It's Fine. It's Fine. It's... Fine?

Zora didn't do anything wrong.

I keep saying that to myself, like maybe if I say it enough, the weird ache in my chest will go away.

She waved at me in the hallway. She complimented my shoes. She even held the door open for me when I dropped my water bottle on the way into science.

It's fine. We're fine. Totally, completely fine.

Except I didn't sit with her at lunch today. I couldn't.

I sat at the edge of the library window and ate my sandwich while pretending to look busy on my Chromebook. I told myself I wanted the quiet. I needed to catch up on an assignment. But really... I just didn't want to sit next to her and pretend everything felt the same.

Because it doesn't.

I wanted to talk about the dance. Yesterday, I did. I really did. Now, I don't know.

I keep thinking—what if she already has a plan? What if she wants to go with her math group?

What if I bring it up and she says, "Oh, I didn't think you'd want to go." That last one might break me.

Anyway.

I folded up the invitation flyer I found taped to my locker and stuffed it in my pocket.

I'll ask her about it tomorrow. Maybe.

Probably.

Or maybe I won't.

It's fine. (It's not.)

—Maya

*Friday evening, sitting on the rug in Zora's room, soft music is playing in the background, like it knows we're tired.*

# Just Zora Things

I didn't say anything to Zora about lunch the other day.

Not on purpose. I just couldn't figure out how to bring it up without sounding dramatic or needy. She hadn't done anything wrong. And I didn't want her to feel like she had to fix something.

But today after school, she said, "Wanna come over?" like she always does when she knows I need it.

I said yes.

We didn't talk about lunch or feelings or anything serious. We ate microwave popcorn and sorted her stickers by color because she likes doing that when her brain's tired. Mine was tired too.

And then, out of nowhere, she said, "I don't like sitting with other people as much." I blinked at her.

She didn't explain. Just peeled the backing off a jellyfish sticker and stuck it on the back of my hand like it belonged there.

I didn't say anything.

But in my head, I whispered: *Thank you for noticing.*

Zora's not the kind of friend who gives long hugs or big speeches.

She's the kind of friend who remembers what my silence means. And gives me stickers instead.

I think that might be even better.

Before I left, she handed me one of the dance flyers. I must've made a face because she said, "I'm not going without you."

That one sentence did more than a million hugs.

I don't know if I'm actually brave enough to go. But if I do... I know who I'm going with.

—Maya

*Monday afternoon, I'm in my room with the door shut, pretending to do homework but mostly just staring at my ceiling fan.*

# The Normal Family Project

In Social Studies today, Mr. Lewis handed out a new assignment called the "My Family Tree Project." It's one of those "fun" things teachers give before a long weekend, like they think everyone's home life is made of movie nights and matching pajamas.

We're supposed to make a poster with pictures and stories about our family—traditions, favorite foods, vacations, holidays, stuff like that. He called it "a celebration of where we come from."

Everyone else acted like they couldn't wait to start.

Noah said he's going to put his dog in every photo, even though it's not technically a person. Marissa talked about karaoke nights. Someone else said their family hikes together every fall and takes goofy leaf photos. The kind you'd see on a Christmas card.

I just sat there and stared at the worksheet. I couldn't even start filling it in.

Because what am I supposed to say?

That we don't eat dinner all together anymore because Benji can't handle too many voices at once?

That we don't go on vacations because even a one-night hotel stay makes him spiral for three days?

That we open gifts in shifts so the wrapping paper crinkling doesn't overwhelm him?

That Mom once cried on Thanksgiving because she accidentally used the wrong brand of mashed potatoes and Benji refused to come downstairs?

What kind of tree does that go on?

And worse: What if I want something *different* sometimes?

What if, deep down, I wish we were the kind of family that had inside jokes and bonfires and messy, noisy game nights? The kind of family that could just be normal for five minutes without everything being about keeping one person okay?

And what kind of awful sister does that make me?

After school, I asked Mom if she could help me brainstorm ideas for the project. She said, "In a bit," because Benji was upset about something with the microwave again. I

didn't even argue. I just nodded and walked out of the room like a background character in my own life.

I know it's not her fault. Or his.

But today it felt like no one remembered I'm part of this family, too.

I'm tired of being the quiet one. The "easy" one. The one who keeps it together while everyone else gets to fall apart.

I want someone to say:

"Hey Maya. Your story matters, too." But no one did.

So now I'm supposed to make a poster about my family. And I don't even know what to put on it.

—Maya

*Tuesday evening, in the laundry room with the door closed, it smells like fabric softener and hot socks.*

# The Laundry Room

I didn't mean to cry today.

I wasn't planning it or anything. It just kind of happened.

Benji had another hard morning. The microwave beeped twice instead of once. Then the cereal wasn't poured yet when he sat down, which apparently *ruined everything.* He started pacing and biting his hand, and Mom ran over like it was a fire.

I was standing right there with my backpack on, ready to go. I had been up early. Got dressed without being told. Brushed my teeth. Found both my shoes. No one said anything. Not "good job," not "thank you," not even "hi."

They didn't mean to ignore me. I know that. It's just that Benji's needs are louder than mine.

They *have* to pay attention to him.

I don't even blame them anymore. It's just how things are.

Mom asked me to take the towels out of the dryer, and something inside me just snapped. Not in a yelling kind of way. Just this small, collapsing feeling, like when a balloon deflates without popping.

So I came in here, sat on the floor, and closed the door. I didn't even do the towels yet. I just sat.

At first, I was just breathing weird. Then the tears started. Quiet ones. I didn't sob. I didn't want anyone to hear. That's the thing—I still didn't want to make it a big deal. Even in my own sadness, I'm trying to take up less space.

I cried into a pair of clean jeans. Not on purpose—it's just what was on top of the basket. I laughed a little after, because what kind of person cries into pants? But it wasn't really funny.

I don't even know what I was crying *about* exactly. Not just this morning.

It was everything. All of it. The way I'm always fine. The way people always say how "strong" I am. The way I feel is as if I *wasn't* strong, the whole house would tip sideways.

I don't want to be dramatic. I don't want anyone to worry about me.

But sometimes I wish someone would come find me in the laundry room and say, "Hey. You don't have to hold everything together."

But no one came in.

So I folded the towels.

And now I'm writing this here.

Because at least the page doesn't talk over me.

—Maya

*Wednesday, on Zora's front porch, her mom's out back gardening, her house always smells like bread and cinnamon, even when no one's cooking anything.*

# Quiet with Zora

I didn't even plan to come here.

I just kind of... showed up. Zora opened the door like she already knew I was coming. She didn't ask questions. She just handed me a glass of lemonade and led me out to the porch like we'd made an appointment or something.

We sat in the squeaky wicker chairs and watched her dog try to catch bees. I didn't talk much. She didn't either.

I think that's what I love most about Zora. She doesn't *push*.

She doesn't ask, "What's wrong?"

She doesn't say, "You can tell me anything," like she's waiting for a big secret.

She just *sits with me,* like I don't have to be interesting or funny or fine to be worth the space I take up.

At one point, she passed me a box of sidewalk chalk. We didn't say anything. Just started drawing on the porch step. I made a star that turned into a cat. She made a spiraling sun with a smiley face inside. I drew a tree that leaned sideways.

It felt stupid and perfect.

And I didn't cry, but I wanted to. Not because I was sad. Just because it felt so *safe*.

I didn't tell her about the Family Tree Project.

I didn't tell her about almost saying something to Mr. Lewis, or about crying in the laundry room, or about how I sometimes wish Benji had been born into someone else's family so I could have a normal one and then feel *less terrible* for thinking that.

I didn't say any of that.

But I think Zora knew anyway.

Sometimes the people who really get you don't need the words. They just hand you chalk and let you draw lopsided trees while your heart works itself out in quiet.

And maybe that's enough for today.

—Maya

*Thursday afternoon. Writing in the nurse's office because I said I had a stomachache. It's not my stomach.*

# Almost

So... I went back to that stairwell at school. The one Benji said was "too loud" and "wrong."

I know it sounds dumb. I mean, it's a floor. Floors aren't supposed to be anything except... there. But ever since he said it, I couldn't stop thinking about it. The way he stood there frozen, like something under his feet was alive. The way he wouldn't move until someone basically dragged him away.

So after the last period, I told Zora I had to grab a paper I dropped and took the long way down. The hallway was almost empty. The light in that stairwell is weird—sort of flickery, even though it's not broken.

I walked down one step at a time, slowly. I didn't know what I was looking for. I just... wanted to *feel* what he felt.

And you know what? It did feel different.

Not broken. Not dangerous. Just... strange. Like the floor had a tiny echo, or like the air was heavier right there. When I jumped a little (just once), the floor gave a tiny bit under my feet. I think. Maybe I imagined it.

It's probably nothing.

But also, why did Benji notice it?

He doesn't lie. He doesn't make stuff up. His brain just *notices* things no one else sees. Sometimes that's annoying, like when he counts my spaghetti noodles or tells me my shoelaces are uneven. But sometimes it makes me wonder...

What else is he picking up that we all miss?

I'm not saying I believe the floor is broken. But something about it has Benji's brain *buzzing*. That usually means something's off—even if the rest of us can't feel it yet.

It wasn't the first time I wondered if Benji and I were feeling the same thing without saying it. I don't know what to do about that.

So for now, I'm just writing it down.

And maybe I'll go back again tomorrow. Just to be sure.

—Maya

*Friday night, in the bathroom with the door locked, I already brushed my teeth, but I'm still in here; it's the only door in the house that no one opens without knocking first.*

# It's Not His Fault, But It Still Hurts

Benji had a hard day.

And by "hard," I mean the kind of day where the whole house rearranges itself to keep him from breaking. The toaster burned the bread this morning, which started it. The smell set him off. Then the sound of the vacuum, even though it was two rooms away. Then Mom put the couch cushions back in the wrong order.

It just kept stacking.

He started rocking. Humming loudly. Flapping his hands so fast they blurred. He knocked over the bin of board games and then curled up on the carpet, holding his ears and sobbing like the world was on fire.

And the worst part?

I didn't even flinch.

Because I'm used to it.

Mom sat beside him, whispering things that wouldn't stick. Dad ran upstairs to get the weighted blanket. I picked up the game pieces and put them back in the box. Then I went into the kitchen and cleaned up the toast.

No one told me to.

No one said thank you either. It's just what I do.

I'm the one who moves around the meltdown.

And I get it—I really do. It's not like Benji wants to fall apart. He doesn't *want* to scream because a cushion is turned the wrong way. He doesn't *try* to take up every ounce of air in the house.

But even when I understand it...

Even when I love him with my whole heart... Even when I know it's not his fault...

It still hurts.

It hurts to watch my parents pour everything into keeping one person afloat and never notice I'm standing in the same water, quietly treading.

It hurts to do all the right things and still feel invisible.

And today it hurt even more.

Because I was supposed to go shopping with Mom—to find something to wear to the dance.

We talked about it earlier this week. She even said it would be fun.

But after everything with Benji, she was too tired. Too stressed. Too gone.

She didn't even mention the family tree project I need help with.

It's due next week, and I still don't know which version I'm going to turn in.

She's not mad.

She's not ignoring me on purpose. She's just not there.

Not for me.

And I don't want to be selfish. I don't want to add one more thing to her already-heavy arms.

But sometimes I wonder if I even matter to my own family. Not in the *"we love you"* way. I know they love me.

I mean in the *"you need something, so I'll show up"* way.

Because I needed her today. And she didn't show up.

I don't want to be angry at Benji. I *don't*.

But sometimes I wish someone would ask if I'm okay—not because something is wrong with *him*, but because something might be wrong with *me*, too.

But no one asked.

So I'm writing it down instead. I'm not trying to be dramatic.

I just want to matter out loud.

—Maya

# Quiet for Once

This afternoon felt… still.

Benji was outside before I was, sitting in the patch of sunlight near the fence. He wasn't lining things up or counting or rocking. He was just running his fingers through the grass like he was feeling every blade one at a time.

I sat a few feet away on the back step. Not because anyone asked me to watch him. Just because the air felt nice — warm but not hot, a little breeze, the kind that makes the leaves flutter without going anywhere.

For a long time, nothing happened. No yelling.

No rushing.

No fixing.

Benji picked up a small yellow leaf and held it up toward the sun. Then he set it down gently beside him, like it was something important. He didn't say anything, and I didn't either.

It didn't feel like a moment I had to manage. It just felt… normal.

Quiet in a good way.

I didn't even realize how much I needed that.

—Maya

*Monday evening, sitting on the edge of my bed with the lights off, I didn't turn them off to sleep—I just didn't feel like being seen.*

# The Cafeteria

Today was horrible.

Not just bad. The kind of day that sticks. That doesn't wash off in the shower or go away when someone says, "It'll be okay."

Benji's aide was out sick. She's the only one who really knows how to get him through a school day without falling apart. So the school sent in a substitute—a nice lady, I guess, but she had no idea what she was walking into.

I don't even know what triggered it.

Too much noise, probably. Or someone moved his tray. Or maybe it was the flickering light over the lunch line. It could've been anything, honestly.

All I know is this:

I was in science class, about to start an experiment, when the office called my name over the intercom. "Maya Thomas to the cafeteria, please."

Everyone looked at me.

And I already knew what it was.

By the time I got there, it was chaos.

Benji was on the floor, wailing. His arms were flapping hard, and he was kicking at anyone who got close. A carton of chocolate milk had exploded on the ground. The substitute aide was standing off to the side, wide-eyed and panicked. Kids were staring. Some were laughing.

Laughing.

And the moment I walked in, the vice principal looked at me like I was the solution. Like I was the *fix*.

I shouldn't know how to handle that situation. I shouldn't be the one they call to *fix it*.

But I did it. Of course I did. I crouched down, used the voice Mom taught me, held out his fidget cube like a peace offering, didn't touch him, just stayed close. After a few minutes, he crawled into my lap and curled into a ball.

And we just sat there. On the cafeteria floor. In front of *everyone*.

Afterward, the staff said things like "Thank you, Maya" and "You really saved the moment." Someone even said I was "amazing."

But I didn't feel amazing. I felt like disappearing.

Like I wanted to unzip my skin and step out of my life for just one second. To be a kid. A regular one. One who doesn't have to calm down her screaming brother in front of the whole school while everyone watches like it's a circus.

I love Benji.

But today I wish I didn't have to be the person he needs all the time.

I wished I could just be me, without also being his translator, his anchor, his emergency contact.

And then I felt horrible for even thinking that because he didn't ask for this either.

I keep replaying the moment he wrapped his arms around my waist and buried his face in my hoodie. Like, I'm the only safe place he has.

And I wonder if I'll ever feel safe, too.

—Maya

*Tuesday night, sitting on Zora's porch steps, porch light is on.*

# After

I went to Zora's after school. I didn't want to go home yet. She opened the door, put a blanket on my shoulders, and we sat outside. Her dog rested its head on my knee.

I kept seeing the cafeteria in my head. The spilled milk. The kids staring. Benji on the floor. Me on the floor. I felt stuck.

She didn't try to fix it. She didn't say the kind of things adults say, like "you're so strong" or "you did the right thing." She just sat with me and breathed slow, which somehow made me breathe slowly, too.

I told her I felt two things at once:

Proud I could help Benji, and embarrassed that I had to do it in front of everyone. Both true. Both big. She said that was okay.

She asked if there's any adult at school who knows *me*, not just "Benji's sister." I said maybe the nurse, maybe my English teacher. I said I'd think about telling one of them how today felt—for me.

We drew with chalk for a while, the way we always do when words run out. She made a sun. I started making squares that turned into a staircase without meaning to. I wiped it away and drew a cloud instead.

- What I know tonight:
- I'm good at calming Benji.
- I shouldn't be the emergency plan.
- I can love him and still hate being watched.
- Two things can be true.

Before I left, Zora gave me a brownie wrapped in a napkin. She didn't make it a big deal. I put it in my pocket. It made me feel seen.

I'm still embarrassed. I'm still tired. But I don't feel alone.

That helps.

As I was putting my shoes on to leave, Zora asked, "Are we still going to the dance?"

I think I just blinked at her for a second.

Then she said, *"Mom's taking me shopping this weekend. You should come. Even if we don't dance, we'll still look awesome in sparkly things."*

I didn't say yes right away. But I didn't say no either. And that felt like a beginning.

—Maya

*Wednesday after school, on my floor with my backpack still on.*

# Whispers

Today felt heavy before it even started.

At breakfast, Benji was calm. He lined up his grapes and counted by twos. Mom looked tired. Dad packed my lunch and forgot the fork. No one said anything about yesterday.

School was the hard part.

People stared at me in the hallway. Not mean—just curious, like I'm a sign to read. A few kids whispered. I heard "cafeteria" and my name in the same sentence and pretended I didn't.

I ate lunch in the library with Zora. We didn't talk much. That helped.

Benji's regular aide was back. I saw them from a distance after math. He looked okay. He was tapping his leg and humming. I felt two things again: relief that he was fine, and anger that I was the one who had to hold it together when he wasn't.

A teacher thanked me in the hallway for "helping yesterday." I nodded. I didn't know where to put that word— helping—when I'm also the one who feels wrecked after.

I thought about going to the nurse to tell her I needed a quiet place. I even stood outside the door for a minute. I didn't go in. I just breathed, counted to twenty, and kept walking. Maybe next time.

After school, I started the Family Tree poster and stared at the empty paper. I wrote our last name at the top and erased it. I don't know if I'm supposed to draw the family I have or the one I wish for. Maybe both are the truth, and that feels wrong.

Here is what I wrote on a sticky note and stuck inside my binder:

- I am not the emergency plan.
- I am allowed to be tired.
- I can love Benji and still not want an audience.
- I get to ask for help.

I don't know who to ask yet.

But writing it down felt like the first step.

—Maya

# The Not-Normal Stairwell

I wasn't planning to go near the big stairwell today. I really wasn't. It had been days since I first noticed it, and it still didn't feel right.

But after the last bell, I saw Benji and his aide at the end of the hall. He was walking fine, then stopped before the stairs like there was an invisible line on the floor. He didn't touch his ears. He didn't flap. He just... paused. Then he turned and took the long way around.

I pretended I needed a drink from the fountain and went closer.

It was normal-looking. Tiles. Railings. Posters on the wall about spirit week. But when I stepped on one tile near the middle, the sound under my shoe felt different—kind of hollow, like tapping an empty box instead of a table. Two tiles over, it sounded normal again.

I put my hand on the rail. It had a tiny buzz in it, not like electricity, more like when a truck goes by far away. I waited. It came and went in a rhythm— soft... pause... soft... pause. I counted. About every twenty-five seconds.

It didn't feel scary. It just felt *wrong* for a floor.

There was a hairline crack near the wall, I swear wasn't there last week. Super thin, like a pencil line. Also, one corner tile sat a little higher than the others, just enough that a rolling cart would probably bump.

I stood there too long, pretending to tie my shoe, and I got that weird feeling in my chest like before a storm, when the air goes heavy.

Later at home, I tried to ask Benji about it.

I didn't say "stairwell" right away. I just said, *"You took the long way today."*

He didn't look at me. Just lined up his markers by height on the table. Then I said, *"Is there something weird about those stairs?"*

He paused. He pressed one marker down like it was a button. Then he whispered something like "underneath" — or maybe it was "under there." I couldn't tell.

I asked, *"What's underneath?"*

But he hummed and shook his head and reached for a different marker.

I didn't push.

I didn't tell anyone.

I don't even know what I'd say.

I just wrote it down here so it stops spinning in my head:

- Hollow sound in the middle tiles
- Rail buzz that comes and goes (about 25 seconds)

- Tiny crack by the wall
- One tile a little higher
- Benji avoids the whole area without melting down—he just *knows*

I don't want to turn this into a big thing. I'm tired of big things.

But I can't stop thinking: if I can feel it now, what is Benji feeling all the time?

—Maya

*Friday night, sitting on the hallway rug outside Benji's room.*

# Asking Benji

I tried to ask Benji about the stairwell tonight.

Not a big talk. Just us on the floor with his Legos between us. I built a boring little house so he wouldn't feel stared at. I kept my voice low. I didn't make him look at me. I asked simple things—what it feels like there, what he notices, why he turns away.

He didn't answer like a regular conversation. He almost never does. But he answered in Benji ways.

He touched his ear and winced a little.

He pressed his palm flat to the carpet and pushed down, then lifted it like something gave under his hand.

He traced a thin line across the floor with one finger, very straight, like a crack.

He tapped the wall in a slow rhythm—pause—tap—pause—tap. I counted in my head. Around twenty-four... twenty-five seconds between the tiny taps.

He put my hand on the heating vent for a second, then moved it away and shook his head. Not hot exactly. Just not the same.

He drew a little box on a sticky note and shaded in one corner darker than the rest, then slid it to me without looking up.

When I asked if he was scared, he didn't nod or shake his head. He just picked up his fidget and squeezed it fast, then slower, then stopped. I took that as a yes-but-not-panic kind of answer.

I told him (quietly) that I'm listening. I don't know if that helped, but he went calmer after, and started lining up the blue Legos by shade.

Here's what I think he told me, without words:

- Sound: there's a low, repeating buzz/pulse that bothers his ears.
- Feel: the floor has a small give in one spot—feels "wrong" underfoot.
- Sight: a very thin line (crack) by the wall; one area looks darker.
- Timing: the weirdness comes and goes about every 25 seconds.
- Heat: there is something a little warmer than it should be.
- Choice: he isn't melting down anymore—he just won't use that stairwell.

I didn't push. I didn't tell him what I think. I just said goodnight in the doorway and left the sticky note on my desk so I won't lose it.

I wish I could speak "Benji" better. But tonight felt like a beginning.

After I brushed my teeth, I found Mom folding towels in the hallway. I told her Zora and her mom invited me to go shopping this weekend, to get something for the dance.

She looked surprised, like she forgot the dance was even happening. Then I saw it—the guilt flood over her face.

She said, "Oh, honey... I wanted to take you. I really did. But I just don't think I can swing it this weekend. Dad's on shift, and Benji's therapy hours changed. I don't want you to miss out, though."

She opened her wallet and handed me two folded twenties. "Here. Get something special. You deserve it."

I said thanks. I put the money in my pocket. But the thing I wanted most wasn't the money.

I wanted her to say, *"Don't go with Zora's mom. I want to take you."*

I wanted her to say, *"This is your first dance. Let's make it a memory."*

But she didn't.

And I didn't ask her to.

I just stood there for a second, holding clean towels I didn't need. Then I went to my room.

I'm grateful. I really am.

But something small in my chest folded in a way I don't think she noticed.

—Maya

*Sunday night, kitchen table, glue stick lid rolling around.*

# Two Trees

We finally sat down to start the Family Tree poster tonight.

Mom brought out a box of old photos and tape. I got the big poster and the markers. We cleared a spot on the table, even though it was already covered in mail and a bowl of apples and Benji's number cards.

We picked pictures first—baby ones, school ones, the one where Dad has flour on his nose. It was nice for about three minutes.

Then Benji couldn't find his blue fork.

Then he needed the green cup, not the clear one. Then the microwave beeped wrong again.

Mom kept getting up. "One second," "Hang on," "Be right back." I kept smoothing the poster so it wouldn't wrinkle.

While I waited, I drew a small tree in the corner. Simple trunk, a few branches. I wrote "Real" under it. Roots and all. Then beside it I drew another one, a little taller, with lights and a tire swing. I wrote "Wish."

I didn't mean anything mean by it. I was just... telling the truth on paper.

Mom came back and saw them. She didn't say anything. She just stood behind me for a minute, warm and quiet, and put her hand on my shoulder. Not a squeeze. Just there.

Then Benji yelled from the other room, and she went again.

I looked at the two trees for a long time. I almost erased "Wish." Instead, I drew roots under both. The "Wish" tree got tiny roots. The "Real" one got big, messy ones that went off the page.

When Mom finally sat down again, we taped a picture of all of us from last fall. Benji's eyes are closed in it. Mine are, too, but only because I'm laughing.

We didn't finish the poster. It's okay.

I put a little heart between the two trees and closed the marker. Both trees are mine.

Even the messy one. Especially the messy one.

—Maya

*Monday afternoon, on my bedroom floor, a poster spread out like a map.*

# Two Trees, One Class

I decided I'm going to put both trees on my Family Tree poster.

The Real tree is the truth: our loud/quiet house, the careful dinners, the way we do holidays in pieces, Benji's rules, Mom's tired eyes, Dad's jokes that try to fix the air.

The Wish tree is also true: game nights, noisy laughter, candles on cakes, a table where nobody has to count their grapes before they eat them.

I'm proud of both.

But I'm scared to show both.

Not everyone understands what it's like being Benji's sister. Some kids think meltdowns are "bad behavior." Some adults call me "amazing" like I'm a poster, not a person. I don't want pity. I don't want applause. I just want honesty.

I made a list to help me decide how to share:

- Option A: Put both trees out in the open. Say, "This is us. Real and wish."
- Option B: Make the Wish tree a little flap that lifts up. If you open it, you see the wish. If you don't, you still see us.

- Option C: Add a small pocket with a note: "Families can be more than one thing at the same time."
- Option D: Show only the Real tree at school, keep the Wish tree in my journal. (Feels safe, but also like hiding.)

I traced both trees in pencil first. The Real one has big roots that run off the page. The Wish one has smaller roots, but they're there. I drew a tiny heart between them again. It helped.

I keep thinking about what people will say. What if they think I'm being mean to Benji? What if they make a face I have to carry home?

Zora texted and said: "Flap. Do the flap."

She's probably right. A flap feels like a choice. You can look, or not. And I still get to tell the whole story without shouting.

I'm going to try it.

I cut a rectangle of cardstock and taped the top so it opens like a door. On the outside, I wrote:

"Our Family, As It Is."

Under the flap, I drew the Wish tree and wrote: "Our Family, As I Sometimes Hope."

Both are true.

Both are mine.

Both belong to Benji, too—even if he never reads this.

I'm still nervous. My stomach does that elevator drop when I think about standing in front of the class. But I think I'll practice at Zora's tomorrow. Maybe I'll read it to her dog first. He's very supportive.

P.S. I keep thinking about the stairwell. I'm not doing anything about it yet. I just notice it, like Benji. Maybe that's enough for now.

—Maya

*Tuesday after school, lying on my bed, face down, then up enough to write this.*

# Off Task

In English, we were supposed to work on a personal narrative. Quiet writing time. Thirty minutes. Easy.

Except I took out my notebook and my brain slid straight to my M-Plan. I started sketching boxes and arrows in the margin: where to go if I get too full (nurse, library), how to ask (blue sticky note), who to try first (Ms. Patel?).

The plan felt important. The story could wait five minutes. Five minutes turned into most of the block.

I wrote:

- Quiet corner pass?
- Blue sticky = "need 5 min"
- Ask the nurse about the resting chair
- Library at lunch on Thursdays
- Sentence I can say: *I need a minute.*
- Backup: breathe in 4, out 6

I was drawing a tiny door that opened and closed when I noticed a shadow on my desk. Ms. Patel. She tapped the rubric with her finger. Everyone else was writing paragraphs. I had one sentence and a whole page of arrows.

She said my name softly and told me this wasn't planning time for other things. It was writing time. She asked me to put the notebook away and focus.

I nodded. My face went hot. I tried to write. The words felt stuck, like dry toast.

At the end of class, she asked me to stay a minute. She wasn't mean. She just said I seemed distracted and I'd need to finish the narrative for homework. She put a little dot next to my name on her clipboard. It wasn't a big deal, but to me it felt like trouble. I'm the "good kid." I don't get dots.

I walked out feeling dumb. I wasn't trying to blow off the assignment. I was trying to keep myself from melting the way Benji does—just quieter.

I wish I could have said that. I didn't.

I tucked the M-Plan page deeper in my notebook and told myself I'd write the story after dinner. (I did. It's fine. It's about the time Dad burned pancakes and pretended it was "intentional caramelization.")

Still, I keep thinking: I made a plan so I could ask for help at school. And the first time I tried to work on it, I got in trouble at school.

Here's what I'm adding to the M-Plan:

- Only work on M-Plan during study hall or at home.
- Ask Ms. Patel if I can have a blue sticky note signal. (Even writing that makes my hands sweat.)
- If I freeze, I write anything for two minutes. Then breathe. Then try again.

I want to be a good student. I also want to be okay. Maybe both can happen.

Maybe I just need to pick better moments.

—Maya

*Wednesday night, sitting on the kitchen floor because the tile is cool and I'm too wired to sit in a chair.*

# Party, Maybe

My birthday is coming up. I want a party. Like... a real one. Friends, cupcakes, music (not loud), maybe a game. Nothing huge. Just normal.

I asked Mom and Dad tonight.

They didn't say no. But they did the face. The worried one. The one that means Benji.

They're scared of noise, mess, people in the house, and the schedule snapping. I get it. I do. But I also felt that old angry-sad feeling climb up my throat. It's my birthday and I'm already apologizing for wanting it.

I don't want to be unfair. I don't want Benji to melt down. I also don't want to skip having a life until everything is easy—because it won't be.

So I made a Quiet Party Plan. I wrote it on a pink index card and stuck it to the fridge so it looks official.

Quiet Party Plan (Maya 12):

- Guests: 4 friends max (Zora + three).
- Time: 2:00–3:30 (short).
- Place: backyard only (doors open, fresh air, easier exit).

- Noise: no balloons, no poppers, no loud music—just a playlist on low.

- Food: cupcakes (no candles), lemonade, fruit.

- Activities: chalk art, a craft table, and a quiet scavenger hunt.

- Heads-up: I'll text the moms and say it's a calm party.

- Benji's plan: headphones ready; quiet room set up with his favorites; if it's too much, Dad takes him for a drive for 30 minutes.

- Me: I get to be the birthday kid without feeling sorry for it.

I left the card where they'll see it. I'm scared they'll still say no, or "maybe later," which is the same thing.

It makes me feel awful to want something Benji might not handle. It also makes me feel awful to not want him there if it's hard. Both things at once, again.

Zora texted: "We'll make it gentle." I like that word. Gentle party. Gentle plan. Gentle birthday.

I'm trying to believe there's a way to keep Benji safe and make space for me. I'm not asking for fireworks.

I just want cupcakes in the backyard with my friends while the sun is out. Is that too much?

—I hope not

— Maya

*Thursday evening, at the kitchen table with glue on my fingers*

# The List

Mom read my Quiet Party Plan and said yes!

She didn't even pause. Just, "Let's try it." I almost cried from relief. We wrote the time on the calendar and she said she'd help me text the other moms. I hugged her and got glue on her sleeve. Oops.

I finished my Family Tree poster tonight. The flap is on there—"Our Family, As It Is" on top, "As I Sometimes Hope" underneath. I'm nervous to share it at school, but Mom said she likes that I told the truth kindly. That helped.

After that, I started my invite list. I want people who know about Benji and won't make a face if something happens. Four guests max. Zora, of course, and three more.

Here's who I picked and why:

- Zora — best friend, calm, knows Benji, brings quiet on purpose.
- Luca — soft voice, likes drawing, never laughs when people are different.
- Marissa — kind, patient, has a younger cousin on the spectrum; she gets it.

- Amir — loves scavenger hunts, is good at following rules, always asks before touching our dog.

I thought about a few others, but if I have to *worry* about them, they're not party people for this year. I want "gentle," not "prove something."

Mom said the list seems perfect. She also said we'll set up a quiet room for Benji and make it easy for him to choose in or out. I like the words choose in or out. It means he belongs, but he doesn't have to perform.

I'm excited. Also scared. But mostly excited. Cupcakes, chalk, sun, friends.

Please let it be simple.

Oh—and the school dance is this Friday.

I keep forgetting it's so soon, then remembering and getting that swooshy feeling in my stomach.

I'm excited. Really excited.

And nervous. Really nervous.

But there's something else I haven't said out loud—not even to Zora: I feel a little bit glad that Benji's not going.

Not because I don't love him.

Not because I don't want him to have fun things too.

But because this is the first thing that feels like it's just *mine*. No extra plan. No backup plan. No emergency kit in my bag. Just me, going to something, being someone.

And I feel guilty about that. I don't want to be selfish.

But I also want to be allowed to shine, even just for one night. Is that selfish?

I don't know.

But I'm going.

And I hope I glow.

—Maya

*Friday morning, dance day.*

# It Was Supposed to Start Happy

I woke up with butterflies today. The good kind.

The "something big is happening" kind.

I opened my eyes already smiling, which almost never happens.

I actually wanted to talk to Mom this morning—like *really* talk. I wanted to ask her if she thought I should wear my hair up or down. I wanted her to say something like, *"Let's try a few styles."* I wanted us to sit on the edge of her bed and laugh at ourselves for being clueless about hair.

But then... Benji happened.

The toast wasn't cut in the right shape. His socks felt "wrong."

Mom was rushing because she had to start dinner early so Zora and I would have time to get ready after school.

It all just... tipped.

He screamed. He kicked the cabinet. He threw his cereal bowl. And my moment disappeared.

I didn't get to ask.

I didn't even get to say good morning.

I grabbed my backpack, walked out the door, and just kept walking. And here's the part that makes me feel small:

I wasn't even mad at Benji.

I was mad that I let myself believe today could be about me. I know my mom cares.

I know she wants me to be happy tonight.

But sometimes wanting isn't the same as *doing*.

And right now, it feels like everything that's supposed to be special just keeps getting swallowed by the noise.

I wanted today to start happy.

But instead, I walked to school feeling sad, mad, and disappointed... and trying not to let it show.

—Maya

*Friday evening, right before we left*

# Let's Do This

Even though the morning hurt, I wanted tonight to feel different. After school, Zora kept her promise.

She showed up with her tote bag, her playlist, and her calm. She said, *"Let's get ready like we're going to a concert."*

I didn't even realize how much I needed that. I exhaled for the first time all day.

Then we got to my house. Chaos.

Mom was still cooking dinner and talking fast. Dad was trying to find clean socks for Benji. Benji was already melting because dinner was early, and it threw off his routine.

The kitchen sounded like five radios on different stations. Zora and I slipped upstairs.

I closed my bedroom door. Turned on my music.

Turned it up.

Benji's screaming faded a little, but not completely. It never really does. I sat in front of the mirror.

At first, I just stared at my face.

Then I added a little sparkly eyeshadow. Brushed my hair the way Zora showed me. Put on my favorite earrings—the little blue ones.

And then I looked again.

And I actually *liked* what I saw.

I didn't look like someone playing dress-up.

I looked like someone real. Someone going somewhere. Someone becoming something.

I took a deep breath.

Then I smiled and whispered, *"Let's do this."*

We came downstairs just as Dad was grabbing his keys to drive us to school. I stood in the hallway for a second, hoping they'd say something. Hoping they'd notice.

But Benji was screaming again. About his schedule.

About the noise.

About the smell of the food.

I waited anyway. Just in case.

Maybe someone would turn and say, *"Wow, Maya. You look beautiful."*

But no one did.

Zora gently touched my hand. I smiled. Just barely.

And we walked out the door.

—Maya

*Saturday morning, still in pajamas, still smiling a little.*

# Just Me and Dad

I was so tired last night after the dance. My legs were sore from dancing (yes, I danced!) and my cheeks hurt from smiling. I didn't even realize how late it was until we pulled into the driveway.

Mom had a headache and went to bed early. Benji was already asleep. But Dad?

He was waiting for me.

Not just *awake*, but actually *waiting*. Lights still on. Sitting on the couch like he was saving a spot for me.

He asked, *"So? Tell me everything."*

And I did.

We talked for almost half an hour—real talking, not the fast kind where someone nods and checks their phone. He asked what the gym looked like. What music played. Who I danced with. If the cupcakes were any good. (They were.)

He laughed at the story about Zora pretending to ballroom dance with a mop during a slow song. He smiled when I told him I felt kind of... confident like I belonged there.

He didn't rush me. He didn't interrupt. He just listened.

It was the kind of listening that makes you feel like your words matter. Like *you* matter. I didn't realize how much I'd been needing that.

Friday didn't start very well.

But the ending—at home, with Dad—just Maya and Dad— It made my heart sing.

—Maya

*Sunday evening, sitting in my room, flipping through old birthday photos.*

# What I Want and What I Know

So I made a list today.

"What I Want My Party to Be Like." It had things like:

- Music loud enough to dance
- Glow sticks
- Nachos (real ones with jalapeño cheese)
- Silly string
- Staying up late
- Everyone laughing and no one crying

Then I made another list.

"What I Know My Party Will Actually Be Like." That one had:

- Volume limits
- No balloons (too poppy)
- Short time frame
- Benji's headphones at the ready
- Mom checking in every five minutes
- Me watching everyone's reactions instead of just *being there*

It felt unfair while I was writing it. Still does.

But then I remembered something from counseling:

Just because something is hard doesn't mean it's bad.

Just because it's different doesn't mean it's not worth doing. Still... it's hard.

I want a party that doesn't have rules. I want a party that feels like *mine*.

And at the same time—I want Benji to be okay.

And I want Mom not to be stretched so thin she forgets to breathe.

And I don't want to ruin everything by being too much or wanting to be too loud. But I think I still want it anyway.

So maybe the list I really need is:

"What Can I Do to Make This Party Mine, Even With All the Rules?" I'm going to start that one tomorrow.

—Maya

*Monday afternoon, sitting on the floor with a pen, a fresh page, and three different color markers.*

# The M-Plan

Okay. Here's what I came up with.

Maya's Party Plan (aka The M-Plan)

*aka how to still have a real birthday even if it has to be a little bit "modified."*

1.  Lights, but not loud ones

    Zora has those soft string lights in her room—the warm kind that don't flash. She said we could use them in the backyard. It'll feel cozy, like a movie scene without being overstimulating for Benji.

2.  Craft station instead of chaos

    Instead of a bunch of noisy games, we'll do a chill crafting table. Something that gives people something to do with their hands. Zora says we can make little "wishing jars." Everyone writes a wish and decorates a mini jar. Benji might even like that.

3.  Music on a playlist, not speakers

I'll make a playlist ahead of time. Nothing jumpy or bass-heavy. Just good, calm-but-happy songs. I'll ask everyone to keep the volume low. No phones blasting TikToks.

4.   Set a time limit that works

Two hours. Not too long, not too short. Gives me something to look forward to, and Benji a plan he can count on.

5.   Plan a Benji break

Dad said he could take Benji out for part of the party—maybe a drive or a walk. We'll set it up so he doesn't have to be there for the whole thing unless he wants to be.

6.   Only invite people who won't make it weird

This one is hard, but important. No random classmates. Just the ones who *get it*. The ones who won't stare or whisper or treat Benji like a problem. So far: Zora, Amir, Luca, and Marissa.

I still don't know if the party will turn out the way I want. But now it feels possible.

And that's better than before.

—Maya

*Tuesday night, kitchen table, papers everywhere.*

# IEP Papers

Mom spread out a stack of school papers after dinner. Benji's name was on every page. She said they were for his IEP meeting this week. (That's his plan at school—the one that says what helps him.)

There were words I see a lot now:

- sensory
- transitions
- visual schedule
- breaks
- noise-canceling headphones
- preferred seat
- prompt and wait time
- self-regulation

I got a highlighter and asked if I could help. Mom said yes without looking up. Dad read quietly and tapped a pen.

I skimmed the goals. They sounded like this:

- Use words or a card to ask for a break.
- Move from one class to the next with fewer prompts.
- Tolerate fire drill with support.

- Join group work for three minutes, then five. There was a page called Accommodations.

It listed:

- Headphones when it's loud
- A quiet corner
- Extra time
- Visual steps for tasks
- Adult to model a calm voice
- Safe person to go to

I felt two things again: helpful and left out. I'm glad he has a plan. I also wish I had one. While they talked, I made a tiny plan for me on a sticky note. I called it "M-Plan."

M-Plan (draft):

- Quiet place: library, nurse, or Zora's porch (after school).
- Safe person at school: maybe the nurse… or Ms. Patel (English).
- Signal: Hand the teacher a blue sticky note if I need a five-minute break.
- One thing that's mine: Friday art club or reading in the library at lunch once a week.
- Home: a door I can close without feeling guilty.
- Words I can say: "I need a minute," "I'm not okay yet," "Please ask me what I need."

- Goal: Ask for help one time each week, even if it's small.

I didn't show Mom and Dad. Not because it's a secret. I just wanted it to be real for me first.

Benji came by and lined up three paperclips and left again. Mom kept reading. Dad asked about "supports during lunch." I looked at all the pages with Benji's name at the top and felt proud. Then I looked at my sticky note and felt steadier.

I don't need an official meeting. But I need a plan. I folded the sticky note and slid it into this journal. It's not an IEP.

It's just... how I'm going to take care of me.

—Maya

*Wednesday, after school, on my bed, a poster rolled up with a rubber band.*

# Not the Only One

I presented my Family Tree today.

I was shaking before it was my turn. My hands felt sweaty on the poster. I almost kept the flap closed and just said normal stuff, but I didn't. I took a breath and told the truth.

I showed the Real tree first. I said our house is sometimes quiet-on-purpose, that we eat in shifts, that we don't do candles, that my brother Benji needs things a certain way. I said we still laugh. I said we are still a family.

I didn't look at anyone's face while I talked. I just looked at the paper. When I finished, I waited for the weird silence. It didn't come.

Kids started raising their hands. One by one.

They didn't ask questions to poke holes. They shared.

- Someone said their parents are divorced and holidays are split, and it's hard but okay.
- Someone said their little sister has diabetes, so birthdays are different at their house, too.
- Someone said their dad works nights and sleeps during the day, so they have to be quiet all the time.

- Someone said their grandma moved in and forgets things, and dinner takes longer now.
- Someone said their family doesn't celebrate certain holidays, and people make comments.
- Someone said money is tight and vacations are pictures on a screen for now.
- Someone said their cousin is autistic and they use headphones at Thanksgiving.
- Someone said their baby brother screams at loud noises, and they hate fire drills too.

It kept going. Not dramatic. Just honest.

I felt my shoulders drop. I didn't know I'd been holding them up so high.

At the end, I pointed to the flap and said there's a "wish" tree under it. I didn't open it. I just said it exists. Mr. Lewis nodded like that was enough.

After class, Luca told me he liked my roots. He meant the ones I drew. He said they looked strong.

I walked to my locker lighter. Not because my life changed, but because my place in it felt less lonely.

Here's what I learned today:

- Telling the truth kindly is a kind of courage.
- Lots of families are "not normal" in quiet ways.
- You can share just enough and still keep some things for yourself.

- I'm not the only one.

I rolled up my poster and brought it home. I think I'll hang it in my room for a while. Both trees. Both true.

—Maya

*Thursday night. On the couch under the blanket. TV's on, but I'm not watching it.*

# The List That Matters

Today I gave out my party invitations. Not paper ones—just quiet, folded notes I wrote on pastel index cards. Simple. Nothing that would draw too much attention.

But still, it felt huge. Like saying, *This is my life, and you're invited into it.*

Here's who I gave them to, and why:

## Zora.

Obviously. She's my whole anchor sometimes. She already knows everything—about Benji, about me. She doesn't treat me like I'm fragile or like I have to be strong all the time, either. She just... gets it.

## Amir.

He's not super talky, but he notices things. Last week in science class, he moved seats when Benji needed more space. Didn't even make a big deal about it. Just scooted over and kept working. I trust that kind of quiet.

**Luca.**

He's funny in a calm way, not the kind that takes up the whole room. He's creative, and he makes people feel comfortable without even trying. He once sat next to Benji at recess and just drew a city out of chalk without saying a word. Benji ended up drawing beside him. No meltdown. No weird looks.

**Marissa.**

She's gentle. And she doesn't ask too many questions when I'm tired. She always seems to know when I need space—and when I don't.

That's it. Four people.

Four people who I think could handle a Maya-style party. One that might get interrupted or go quiet all of a sudden or require extra kindness without warning.

Zora grinned and said, "I'm bringing glitter glue." Luca smiled and asked if he could bring a sketchbook for the chalk art ideas. Marissa said, "That sounds perfect," and Amir gave me a high-five and said he's good at scavenger hunts.

So it's happening.

My birthday. A real party. Just five of us, including me. It should feel exciting. And it does... but also not.

Because every time I try to plan a detail, there's a list of "can't" right behind it.

- Can't have balloons → too loud if one pops.
- Can't have candles → Benji can't handle fire or the singing.
- Can't play music loud → sound hurts him.
- Can't shout "surprise" or be silly too long → unpredictability = meltdown.
- Can't have a long party → he gets overwhelmed after a while.
- Can't have chocolate cupcakes → the smell bothers him.
- Can't play tag or running games → too much movement, too fast.

Every time I say, "What if we..." someone (usually Mom or me) says, "Well... maybe not."

And it's not fair to Benji. I know that. He didn't ask to have a nervous system that hears and feels everything louder than we do. But still—

I just want to have fun.

I want to laugh too hard. I want to be loud for five minutes. I want to eat a cupcake without checking first if it's "safe." I want to be the center of something without guilt clinging to it like fog.

I feel bad for even writing that. But it's true.

Mom helped me print scavenger hunt cards today and reminded me we need a "Benji Plan" too. Quiet space in his room, headphones ready, a show queued up. Dad said he'll take him for a drive if it gets too much.

I nodded. Said okay. Smiled like a good daughter. But inside, I wanted to yell. It's just two hours.

Can't I have two hours where I don't have to plan around someone else's edges?

I don't want to be ungrateful. I don't want to be unkind.

I just want to feel normal for one afternoon.

I'm scared it's going to be weird.  I'm scared something will go wrong.

I'm scared they'll say yes and still not come.

But I'm also proud I did it.

I asked. I opened the door.

And now I get to see who walks through.

—Maya

*Friday late afternoon, sitting at the desk in my room, the drawing is next to me.*

# The Marker and the Map

Something strange happened today.

During passing period, I was at my locker when I saw a kid from 6th grade—Nina, I think—drop her marker. It rolled across the hallway, right toward the stairwell.

I don't know why I watched it so closely. Probably because it rolled exactly over the part of the floor I've been watching. The marker hit the raised tile—clicked—and then... it was gone.

Not like "behind something." Like into something.

It slid toward the wall, spun once, and disappeared into that thin crack near the baseboard.

Nina looked around but didn't go after it. She just shrugged and pulled out another one. Nobody else even noticed.

I went back there after school. The crack looks wider now. Not a lot. But enough. The grout around one edge looks like it's darkening again, like it's always slightly wet after it rains—even though it hasn't rained in days.

One corner of a tile has a new chip, like maybe someone stepped on it hard. There's still that quiet, buzzy feeling in the rail. I counted again. Twenty-five seconds.

I felt weird after that. Not scared. Just full of too many thoughts. But tonight—Benji gave me something.

He didn't say anything. Just walked into my room while I was doing math and slid a drawing onto my desk. Then he walked out.

At first I thought it was one of his usual patterns, but then I looked closer. It's a grid. Like floor tiles. One square is shaded darker, and there are numbers next to it:

25

25

25

25

He drew a thin line near the side of the shaded tile. There's a tiny wave shape next to it, the kind he sometimes draws when music is "too wobbly" for him. He even taped a blue dot sticker in the corner—his way of saying "watch this spot."

I stared at it for ten minutes.

He's tracking it. The tile. The pulse. The rhythm.

He's been noticing everything I've noticed—and maybe more. He just didn't have the words. So he made a map.

I don't know how long he's been feeling this. I don't know what to do with the drawing.

I don't know who to show.

But now I'm sure.

Something's wrong with that part of the floor. And Benji's known the whole time.

Part of me wants to tell someone.

Part of me is afraid no one will believe me.

Part of me wants to slide the map into my backpack and wait. But I won't forget.

Not the marker. Not the map.

Not Benji trusting me with both.

—Maya

*Sunday evening, lying on Zora's floor, feet on her beanbag, Benji's drawing is in my pocket.*

# Zora Believes Me

I told Zora everything.

I didn't mean to. I just started talking.

We were sitting in her room, half-eating crackers, half-doing homework, and my brain wouldn't stop spinning about the stairwell. So I pulled out the paper Benji drew—the one with the tiles and the numbers—and handed it to her.

She studied it, her brow doing that tiny pinch it always does when she's really thinking. She didn't laugh. She didn't look confused. She just... took it seriously.

I nodded. I told her how a marker rolled across the floor and disappeared into the crack. I told her the buzz in the railing is still there. The dark line is wider. The tile feels warmer. Nobody else notices. And Benji? He's been tracking it. Quietly. In his own way.

I waited for her to laugh or look at me like I was making it up. She didn't.

Zora didn't say much. But she listened the whole time. She didn't try to fix it. She didn't interrupt. And she didn't tell me I was imagining things. That alone made my chest feel a little less tight.

I started to realize I'd been holding this—all of this—by myself for too long. I didn't even notice how much it was weighing on me until I let Zora in. And now that I did, it doesn't feel like a secret. It feels like a question. A problem we need to do something about.

Not because we want attention. Not because it's dramatic.

But because something's wrong, and the grown-ups still aren't seeing it. Now what?

Because here's the thing: I already tried to tell adults before. I told the nurse. I hinted to my teacher. I even left a sticky note once. Nothing changed. Nobody took it seriously.

And I'm scared.

I don't want to be the kid who "makes things up."

I don't want people to look at Benji like he's broken. I don't want to be in the middle of something big.

I just want to be heard.

Zora's reaction reminded me of something important: I'm not crazy for noticing. And I'm not alone. She gets it. She believes me. And somehow, that made me believe myself more, too.

We made a plan:

- Bring the drawing.
- Write down what we've seen—facts only.

- Start with the nurse, because she listens.

- This time, ask her to come *see* it with us.

- No big speeches. Just show them.

I'm nervous.

But Zora believes me.  Benji gave me the drawing.

And now it's not just my worry anymore. That makes it a little easier to carry.

I'm not sure what'll happen next. But we're going to try.

—Maya

October 31st



# Trick, Treat, Change, Repeat

We don't really *do* Halloween at my house.

Not because we don't like it—well, *I* like it—but because Benji really, really doesn't.

He doesn't like costumes. He doesn't like masks. He *really* doesn't like the doorbell ringing over and over or voices shouting *"Trick or treat!"* through the screen.

So every year, Mom and Dad keep the porch light off and play white noise in his room. It's easier that way—for him.

And usually, I just stay home too.

But this year, Zora invited me over. She said,

*"You should still get to have a night."*

So I did.

We dressed up in her room—Zora was a forest witch with fake moss on her shoulders, and I was a glittery comet with silver stars in my hair. Her mom took a thousand pictures and told us we looked "ethereal," whatever that means.

We went trick-or-treating on the quieter streets. Zora knew exactly which houses gave out mini chocolates and which ones handed out toothbrushes. We skipped the loud houses and the ones with fog machines.

We laughed. We ran a little. We waved at toddlers in dinosaur suits. It was just... easy.

And fun.

And for me.

Before we walked back to my house, I changed out of my costume in Zora's bathroom. Took off the stars.

Pulled on a hoodie.

Brushed the glitter off my cheeks.

Because walking in dressed like a comet might've thrown Benji off, and I didn't want to end the night with a meltdown.

At home, Mom took my candy bag to "inspect" everything before I could bring it upstairs. (It's the rule. She always sneaks a peanut butter cup. I let her.)

Benji was already asleep. The house was quiet.

The porch light was still off.

I tiptoed upstairs and dumped my candy out on the floor just to look at it. I didn't even want to eat it right away—I just wanted to *see* it.

Tonight wasn't huge.

It wasn't wild.

But it was mine.

And Zora made sure of that. I'm really lucky to have her.

Not just because she lets me be a comet once a year...

But because she understands when I need to change back before going home.

—Maya

*Tuesday after school, kitchen table, planning the party playlist, just the quiet songs.*

# She Saw It

Today I did something big.

I asked the school nurse to come with me to the stairwell.

It took me three tries to say it out loud. I kept walking past her door like I wasn't sure where I was going. But on the third pass, I stepped in and told her I needed to show her something. Not an emergency. Just... something important.

She put her pen down and followed me.

We walked the long way so Benji wouldn't see us. I didn't want him to get anxious about it. When we got to the stairwell, I pointed to the tile. The one near the wall with the dark grout line and the raised edge.

She bent down. Touched the floor with her fingers. Pressed near the crack. Her brow furrowed.

She stood up and looked at me. Then she looked again at the floor. And this time, I could tell—

She saw it.

She didn't say much, just that she was going to "let someone know" and "have it checked out." But it was enough. It was *everything.*

I didn't need a big scene. I didn't need someone to panic. I just needed one adult to *notice* what I noticed.

To believe what Benji felt. To make it real.

Walking back to class, I felt light in my chest. I don't feel that very often.

I'm still thinking about it now while I work on my birthday plans. Saturday is so close. The cupcakes are ordered. Zora's bringing the craft supplies. Luca and Amir already RSVP'd. I made little scavenger hunt cards shaped like stars. Marissa's bringing fruit skewers because "cupcakes aren't fruit."

We're even going to hang string lights in the backyard—even though they're not flashy ones, just the soft glow kind.

Benji has his plan too. Dad's taking him for a drive partway through the party, and his quiet room will be all set up just in case.

I don't know how it's all going to go.

But I'm starting to feel like I can enjoy it. Like it can be mine.

And for the first time in a while, everything doesn't feel too big to hold.

—Maya

*Wednesday night, sitting on my bed with a blanket around my shoulders, everything feels loud, even though the house is quiet.*

# After the Fall

Someone fell on the staircase today.

I don't know who. I didn't see it happen.

All I know is, right after the third period, the hallway near the stairwell was full of people. Teachers with walkie-talkies. A cart blocking the stairs. A yellow folding sign that said *"Caution: Floor Under Review."* I heard the word *"slipped"* and *"ankle"* and *"wet spot"* more than once.

No one said a name. The crowd thinned fast. The bell rang like nothing had happened. But something did.

And for the first time, I didn't feel panicked. I didn't feel frozen or guilty or invisible. I felt… relieved. Not that someone got hurt—never that—but that I told someone. An adult. Someone who listened.

The nurse saw the crack. She touched it. She said she'd let someone know. And maybe she did, and maybe that's why they were finally watching it today. Maybe that's why there was a sign. Maybe the fall wouldn't have been worse because someone was paying attention.

I kept thinking: *What if I hadn't said anything?*

Maybe it would've been brushed off again. Maybe the marker rolling into the floor would've just been a weird thing I noticed. Maybe Benji's drawings would've stayed folded up in my journal. Maybe I would've been scared, and alone with it, forever.

But now... I'm not.

I don't know if they're going to fix the floor. I don't know who got hurt or how bad it was. But someone's noticing. Someone's taking it seriously. And that's enough for today.

The party is in two days.

Zora brought over little paper lanterns that we can hang on the tree branches. She said they glow softly, like "birthday fireflies." Amir texted that he's bringing his old instant camera, and Luca is designing custom chalk art squares for everyone's names.

Mom helped me pick out the tablecloth. We picked yellow. Calm but still sun-shiney. Benji's room is ready with his favorite things, and Dad said he'll drive him to the nature trail if it gets too loud.

I'm still nervous. But now it's a different kind of nervous. Not scared-nervous. Just excited-nervous.

Things feel okay.

And for once, I feel okay, too.

—Maya

*Thursday, people were high-fiving me in the hallway, real high-fives, like, palm-smacking, grinning kind.*

# Me and Benji, the Team

So... apparently everyone knows about the stairwell now.

After the fall last week, and then the facilities guy putting in a repair order, and then someone seeing construction tape up this morning, it kind of turned into a thing. And somehow *my name* got attached to it.

At first, I didn't think anyone would notice. But today? People *noticed.*

The front railing has yellow tape on it now. One whole section of tile is blocked off. There's a sign that says *"Caution: Temporary Closure for Safety Repairs."*

And then, at lunch, kids I barely talk to came over and said stuff like,

*"Hey, you're the girl who found the floor thing, right?"*

*"That's wild. What if someone really got hurt? That's so cool you caught it." "Dude, high five."*

And I mean—*I got high fives.* Multiple.

I was kind of stunned. I just nodded and said, *"Thanks,"* like I get safety compliments every day.

Then, in class, my teacher actually paused while handing back homework and thanked me. She told me that if I hadn't spoken up, more students could have been hurt. She even said that she was really proud of me!

And my face turned red like a tomato. But in a good way.

I waited until everyone went back to their papers, and then I told her that it wasn't just me that it was Benji, too.  I told her that he noticed it first and that we kind of worked as a team.

She smiled at me like the kind of smile that makes your chest warm. Even better, she told me to tell Benji thank you from her.

So yeah.

Today, I wasn't just *Benji's sister.*

I wasn't invisible.

I wasn't walking around someone else's meltdown.

I was Maya.

The girl who paid attention. The one who listened.

The one who helped.

Me and Benji.

The team.

And I think that's worth remembering.

—Maya

*Friday after school, back to reality.*

# The Lunch Table Promise

Today at lunch, I sat with Zora like always, but I was quieter than usual. She noticed.

I was picking apart my sandwich and staring at the dots on my lunch tray when she asked me what was wrong.

I tried to brush it off at first. I said I was *fine.*

She gave me that look that means, *"Try again."*

So I told her.

I told her the truth—that I'm nervous about the party. Not the cupcakes or the games or even whether people will like the scavenger hunt. I'm nervous about *Benji.*

What if he gets overwhelmed?

What if he screams in front of everyone?

What if someone says something mean, or looks uncomfortable, and the whole mood shifts?

What if *this one thing* that's supposed to be for me ends up being about him again?

Zora didn't say anything right away.

She just nodded, like she was really listening. Then she stood up.

She turned around and waved over to where Luca and Marissa and Amir were sitting. I panicked for a second—I didn't want her to make a big deal out of it.

But she didn't.

She just asked them to come over to our table. They came over without asking why.

We sat together—like, close—so we could whisper, and Zora told them I'm nervous about how things might go with Benji.

Nobody laughed.

Nobody made a weird face. Nobody even looked surprised.

Amir said his cousin is like Benji, so he had practice. Luca said he likes quiet parties better anyway.

Marissa said if he needs a break, we'll give him space and if I need a break, they've got me.

And right there in the cafeteria, over half-eaten sandwiches and cartons of milk, we all kind of... nodded.

Like we'd signed an invisible contract. It only lasted a few minutes.

The lunch bell rang and everyone scattered again.

But something about that little circle at the table made my chest feel lighter. I think maybe I don't have to hold this whole party by myself.

I think maybe... it's okay to be held, too.

—Maya

*Friday night, everything's set up, kind of feels like holding my breath.*

# Almost Party Time

Zora came over after dinner just to double-check everything. She said, *"We've got this,"* before she even took her shoes off.

Then she pulled out her mini clipboard with the scavenger hunt list she helped me plan and a pouch full of glow sticks. She even brought backup napkins. Who thinks of backup napkins?

We sat cross-legged on my floor, going over the plan one last time—games, snacks, quiet space for Benji, chalk bucket, playlist. She helped me lay out the craft stuff, and then we both tested the speakers to make sure they weren't "too loud, too sudden."

And honestly? Having her here made me feel a hundred times better. We didn't talk about the *what-ifs.*

Just the *whens.*

We even practiced the cupcake arrangement like it was a science fair. Then—surprise—Mom actually stuck her head in the room.

She didn't look rushed or distracted. Just... present. She smiled and said that everything is going to be okay.

And I didn't realize how badly I needed to hear that until she said it. I just nodded and said thanks, but inside, something *unclenched.*

She didn't promise that nothing would go wrong.

She just let me know that I'm not alone in trying to make it right.

Zora left with a sleepy wave and a *"see you tomorrow, party captain."*

Now I'm sitting here in my pajamas, staring at the string lights I already plugged in. It's happening.

My party. My plan. My people.

Please let it be gentle.

Please let it be fun.

Please let me *remember* it as something that felt like mine.

—Maya

*Saturday night, in my room with cupcake crumbs on my pillowcase and glitter in my socks.*

# The Middle and the Ending

It was my party today.

I woke up early, even though I didn't have to. I triple-checked the scavenger hunt clues and made sure the chalk buckets were labeled. Mom made lemonade and Dad hung the string lights in the trees. Benji stayed in his room, tapping his number cards on the desk like he was counting the hours out loud.

I felt this warm bubble inside—like maybe today would be just... mine. At first, it really was.

Zora got here first, carrying her glitter glue and a bag of puffy stickers. Luca brought

sidewalk chalk so pretty it looked like candy. Marissa helped Mom set the table, and Amir started mapping out a perfect scavenger strategy before I even handed out the clue cards.

Everything felt light and golden until it didn't.

Benji came outside halfway through. At first, it was okay. He stood by the edge of the yard, rocking on his heels, watching the lanterns sway in the wind. I waved. He didn't wave back, but he stayed. That felt like enough.

Then someone—probably Amir—dropped a metal spoon onto a plate. It made a sharp, clattery *clank*. It wasn't loud to me. But for Benji... it cracked something.

He froze.

Then he let out this sharp, thin sound and covered his ears. His whole body stiffened, like he was trying to hold back an earthquake with just his arms.

Mom moved fast. She rushed to him, but it was already too much. Benji started yelling, shaking his head, backing away. Everyone stopped. All my friends. The party paused like someone had hit a button.

And I just stood there.

Cupcake in one hand. Napkin in the other. My birthday happening... and unraveling.

But then something strange and kind happened.

Zora turned the music all the way down. Luca handed me a piece of chalk—just handed it to me like this was normal. Marissa crouched near Benji, not close, just *near*, and quietly started humming the tune he always hums when he's trying to calm down. Amir handed Mom Benji's headphones from the table. He remembered. He noticed.

Benji didn't stop shaking, but he slowed.

He took the headphones. Sat down. Rocked. And the party didn't end.

It just shifted.

We moved to the front yard while Dad took Benji for a drive. We finished the scavenger hunt with whisper voices. Zora made us all crown headbands out of construction paper. Amir took silly Polaroids. Marissa showed me how to make a flower out of tissue paper. Luca drew a chalk mural that said "Maya Day" in big, loopy letters.

And I laughed.

Not fake. Not polite. Real. The kind that reaches your ribs.

Before everyone left, Mom pulled me aside. She didn't give a big speech or anything. Just looked at me for a long time and said that I was amazing today, that she knows it's not always easy for me.

And I don't know why, but that made my eyes sting more than anything else. Because she finally said it.

She finally saw it.

Not just Benji's hard.

Mine, too.

The party wasn't perfect. But it was real.

And mine.

And full of the kind of people who show up and stay. Today, I turned twelve.

And for the first time in a long time, I didn't feel invisible in my own story.

—Maya

*Monday afternoon, sitting on my bed with my shoes still on, something important happened today.*

# They Noticed

Today, after lunch, the school secretary called my name over the intercom.

My stomach dropped, just a little. That always feels like trouble, even when it's not. I zipped up my hoodie and walked down the hall like I wasn't nervous.

There was a man waiting in the front office. He had a clipboard, paint on his sleeves, and a blue ID badge that said "Facilities." The nurse was standing beside him.

He looked at me kindly, not like I was in trouble, just like he had a question.

He asked if I could show him the spot near the stairwell. The one I told the nurse about. So I did.

I walked him over to the tile. I pointed at the edge that still lifts just a little, and the thin crack by the baseboard. He knelt down, tapped the tile lightly, and nodded. Then he asked me how I noticed it. I told him about the sound. The marker. The strange rhythm. He didn't look surprised. Just thoughtful.

He knelt down, tapped it lightly with something metal, then again with his knuckles. He nodded to himself like he already had ideas. He ran his fingers along the rail. I counted to 25 in my head—soft buzz, just like always.

Then he stood up and said, *"You've got a good ear. That's a pressure issue underneath. It could be a leak, maybe a shift in the subflooring. We're putting in a full repair order."*

But then he said something else—quieter this time.

"If you and your brother hadn't noticed this, someone could've really gotten hurt."

And I don't know why, but that sentence hit me straight in the chest. Because he didn't say *Benji* noticed.

He said *you and your brother.*

Me and Benji.

Like we were a team.

Like I helped.

Like I mattered.

And not just to *him*—but to safety. To someone's actual safety. I nodded, trying not to look too proud.

When we walked back toward the office, the nurse smiled at me like she already knew. Like maybe she was proud too.

It was just a short walk. Just a small crack in the tile. But for a second, I felt really tall.

When I got home, my backpack felt lighter.

On my bed was a small white envelope. Just my name on the front. Inside was a card from Mom.

Not long. Not fancy. Just:

"You're not just Benji's sister. You're Maya.

And we're listening now."

No speech. No "I'm sorrys." Just that.

I read it three times. Then I put it in my journal—right next to Benji's drawing of the tile map. The one that started everything.

There are still hard things.

Benji still lines up forks before dinner and flinches when the phone rings. Mom still gets tired.

I still get tired, too.

But something shifted. Someone listened.

Someone noticed.

And now I'm starting to believe that maybe I can be the kind of person who notices *and* still takes up space in the room.

Not just the helper. Not just the quiet one. Just me.

And maybe that's enough.

—Maya

*Tuesday evening, cool breeze through the window, journal open, room quiet.*

# Epilogue

I don't know what I thought being twelve would feel like.

I guess I thought it would be more glittery. More sleepovers. Less complicated. But I think I'm starting to understand that *twelve isn't about everything being easy.*

It's about learning how to stand in the middle of your own story, even if it's a little messy. It's about knowing when to speak up, even when your voice shakes. It's about loving someone who needs a lot—*and* knowing that doesn't mean you need less.

I still have questions. About Benji. About school. About me. But I'm not invisible.

I have friends who notice things.

I have a brother who sees the world in patterns and pulses. I have a mom who's trying.

I have a voice I'm learning to use.

And I have a card tucked into this journal that says I matter. Twelve isn't perfect.

But it's real.

And it's mine.

This is going to be a good year.

—Maya